David Goes to School.

By David Shannon

SCHOLASTIC INC.

New York Toronto London Auckland Sydney
Mexico City New Delhi Hong Kong Buenos Aires

AUTHOR'S NOTE

A few years ago, my mother sent me a book I made when I was a little boy. The text consisted entirely of the words "no" and "David"—they were the only words I knew how to spell—and it was illustrated with drawings of David doing all sorts of things he wasn't supposed to do. I thought it would be fun to do a remake celebrating all the time-honored ways moms say "no." The new version was called No, David!

Well, David's in trouble again. This time it's his teacher saying, "No, David!" It seems that kids haven't changed much over the years, and neither have school rules, some of which date back even farther than the invention of sneakers.

Of course, "yes" is a wonderful word...but "yes" doesn't stop kids from running in the halls.

For Mrs. Harms, Miss Deffert, Mrs. Miller, Mr. Helpingstine,

Mr. Watson, Mrs. Williams, Mr. McDougal, and, of course, Heidi.

This book was originally published in hardcover by the Blue Sky Press in 1999.

ISBN 0-439-32171-9

12 11 10 9 8 7   2 3 4 5 5/0

Printed in the U.S.A.   14

First Scholastic paperback printing, September 2001

David's teacher always said...

NO, DAVID!

No yelling.
No pushing.
No running
in the halls.

David!

$\overline{9}$

$7 + 3 = 10$

14

$+2 =$

Sit down,

$4 + 4 = 7?$

Don't chew
gum in class!

David, raise

Keep your hands

Wait your

turn, David!

David!

Recess is over!

That's it, Mister! You're staying after school!

David, have